On Vacation with Tūtū

Written by **Lynne Wikoff**

Illustrated by **Tammy Yee**

Mutual Publishing

ISBN-10: 1-56647-957-6
ISBN-13: 978-1-56647-957-8
Library of Congress Control Number: 2011933964

Design by Jane Gillespie
First Printing, September 2011

Mutual Publishing, LLC
1215 Center Street, Suite 210
Honolulu, Hawai'i 96816
Ph: (808) 732-1709
Fax: (808) 734-4094
e-mail: info@mutualpublishing.com
www.mutualpublishing.com

Printed in China

For Theo
— L.W.

The sun slipped below the horizon and the
birds settled into their nests.

"Time to clean up your room and then take
your baths, keiki," Mama told Kainoa, Nani,
and little Mehana.

Kainoa pouted. "We don't want to."
Nani pouted. "And we don't want to take a bath."
Little Mehana stomped her foot. "No, no, no."
Mama was not happy.

When the stars twinkled in the sky,
Papa said, "Time to sleep, keiki."
"No, no, no," said Kainoa and Nani
and little Mehana.
Papa was not happy.

The next morning Mama told the keiki, "Papa and I
are going on vacation."

"And while we are away," Papa said, "you'll have
your own vacation right here at home, with Tūtū."

"Yay!" sang the keiki.

Soon, Tūtū arrived. "We're going to have a wonderful time," Tūtū told Akamai, her mynah bird.

Akamai winked.

"Remember, keiki," Papa said, "you must do as Tūtū says."

"Tūtū knows best," squawked Akamai.

Everyone waved goodbye as Mama and Papa went on their way.

When they were out of sight, Tūtū said, "Would you keiki like some ice cream?" "Yay," said the keiki. "We love ice cream."

When they finished, Tūtū said, "Would you keiki like to play outside while I unpack?"
Kainoa and Nani and Mehana happily did what Tūtū said.

"Being on vacation is good fun!" said Kainoa.
"And Tūtū is good fun!" said Nani.
"Fun!" said little Mehana.

By the time Tūtū finished unpacking, the keiki were dirty from head to toe.

"Would you children like to take a bath?" said Tūtū.

"We like being dirty," said Kainoa. "And we're on vacation," said Nani.

"Dirt!" said little Mehana.

"Fine," Tūtū said. "No baths for the whole vacation, okay?"

"Okay!" said the keiki.

Later Tūtū said, "Maybe you should straighten up your room."

"We like our room messy," said Kainoa.
"And we're on vacation," said Nani.
"Mess," said little Mehana.

Tūtū smiled. "No cleaning rooms for the whole vacation, okay?"
"Okay!" sang the keiki.

After dinner, Tūtū said, "Will you be ready for bed soon?"

"We want to stay up," said Kainoa.
   "And we're on vacation," said Nani.
      "Up!" said little Mehana.

Tūtū nodded. "No bedtime for the whole vacation, okay?"
   "Okay!" sang the keiki.

The keiki played and played and played. They didn't clean their rooms and they didn't take their baths and they didn't go to sleep until they dropped from exhaustion. They had so much fun they wanted their vacation to go on forever.

"Tūtū knows best," chirped Akamai.

One morning Tūtū shook the keiki awake. "Time to get up. Your friends will be here soon."

Kainoa, Nani, and little Mehana rubbed the sleep from their eyes. They got up and rummaged through the mess to find their clothes. They gobbled up their breakfast. Then they greeted their friends.

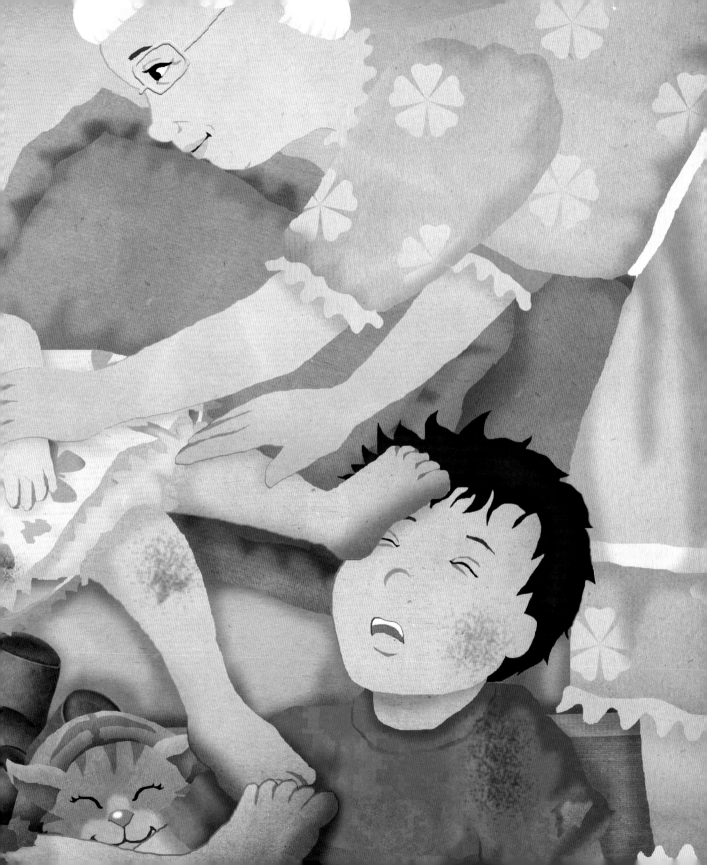

The other kids laughed at Kainoa. "You're wearing your sister's shorts!" They pointed to Nani. "Eeeuw—you have bird poop in your hair!"

They shook their fingers at cranky Mehana.
"Crybaby," they said.

"Playing with you is no fun," the other kids
said as they ran off.

Kainoa, Nani, and Mehana went off to find Tūtū.

"We want to take a bath," Kainoa said.

"I'm afraid not," Tūtū said.

"We want to straighten our room," said Nani.

Tūtū shook her head. "Sorry," she said.

"Nap?" Mehana said.

"Nope," Tūtū said. "We agreed—no baths, no cleaning, and no bedtime for your whole vacation."

Akamai squawked. "Tūtū knows best."

At last, just when Kainoa and Nani and little Mehana were so tired of being messy and stinky and sleepy that they thought they couldn't stand one more day of vacation, Mama and Papa returned.

"Hello, keiki," Papa said.

"We missed you," Mama said.

"Can we take a bath?" said Kainoa.

"And clean our room?" said Nani.

"Sleep?" said little Mehana.

"Of course..." said Mama.

"...you may," said Papa.

"Yay!" sang the keiki.
"We love baths, and tidy rooms, and bedtime."

Akamai winked at the keiki.
"Tūtū knows best," he crowed.